THE YOUNG TEACHER AND THE GREAT SERPENT

Irene Vasco · Juan Palomino

translated by Lawrence Schimel

EERDMANS BOOKS FOR YOUNG READERS

GRAND RAPIDS, MICHIGAN

Finally, after studying for many years, the young teacher was ready for her first assignment. But when she read the name of the place where she was being sent, she was a bit unsettled:

Comunidad Las Delicias, in the Amazon?

She had never heard of it.

She looked it up in an atlas and on the internet. In the end, it was quite clear that she was going to work in the middle of the jungle.

"That's fine. Wherever it is, there will be children who want to read and write and learn geography, science, and math. I'll bring lots of books to show them," she thought.

One Saturday, very early in the morning, the young teacher boarded a bus headed for the Amazon. The journey was very long. She had calculated that it would take around twenty hours. But in the end, it lasted over thirty-two hours because of a narrow highway in bad condition, full of curves, potholes, and bumps.

During the journey, the young teacher shared her food with a kind woman seated beside her, who in turn invited her to sleep at her home before continuing on to Las Delicias.

The young teacher's new friend woke her in the middle of the night, handing the teacher her suitcase and her box of books. "Quick, run! The boat's leaving! The clouds tell of a storm, and if the boat doesn't set off right away, the whirlpools in the river will become very dangerous."

"Boat? What boat? I don't want to sail on the river. I get seasick, and I'm afraid of storms and whirlpools," the young teacher protested while the woman urged her to leave.

On the boat, someone loaned her a plastic tarp to protect her box from the water splashing everywhere. The books, her greatest treasure, journeyed safe and dry.

Seven hours later, the young teacher—damp, exhausted, and frightened—reached dry land.

"Please, can you tell me where the school of Las Delicias is?" she asked the young man who helped her unload her luggage.

"Oh, that's very far from here, in the middle of the jungle! What do you need to do there?" the young man answered her. "I could take you on my motorbike to the trail, but then you'd have to walk. Look for someone who can guide you. You can't go alone—you'd be lost within three steps! Oh! And get yourself some rubber boots for the swamps . . . and the snakes. There are lots of them in the jungle."

Four days after leaving her home, the young teacher
finally arrived in Las Delicias.

It was a lovely place on the banks of the river. In that small enclave lived around fifty Indigenous families. The older folks didn't speak Spanish.

The children
showed her where the tiny
school was. It had no walls—nothing
more than a straw roof that sheltered some chairs
and a blackboard resting against a tree trunk. Determined,
the young teacher improvised a bookshelf for all her books, her
treasures, the only things that made her feel sure of herself. Then the
children accompanied her to her new home: a little room on the hill.

Every day, the young teacher went to the school and taught classes. Her students loved the stories from her books. She read them out loud in the morning, and later the children took them to their homes. They were content to leave with a few books beneath their arms, and the teacher often saw her students exchanging them. She also noticed the mothers and grandmothers looking at the books with curiosity and attention.

One morning the children ran by the school, frightened.

"Teacher, the great serpent is awake! It's dangerous, and the school is right next to the river," they said. And they fled toward the hill.

"Don't leave, we've got a geography lesson!" the young teacher said, trying to get her students to stay at the school.

"Run, Teacher, run! We have to reach the high ground. The great serpent is on its way! It's angry because the colonizers have built all along the riverbank. The rains come from the north. The great serpent woke up, and it's coming this way."

"Great serpents don't exist! Those are legends. Don't go, children. Please, we have a lot to learn today," the young teacher begged.

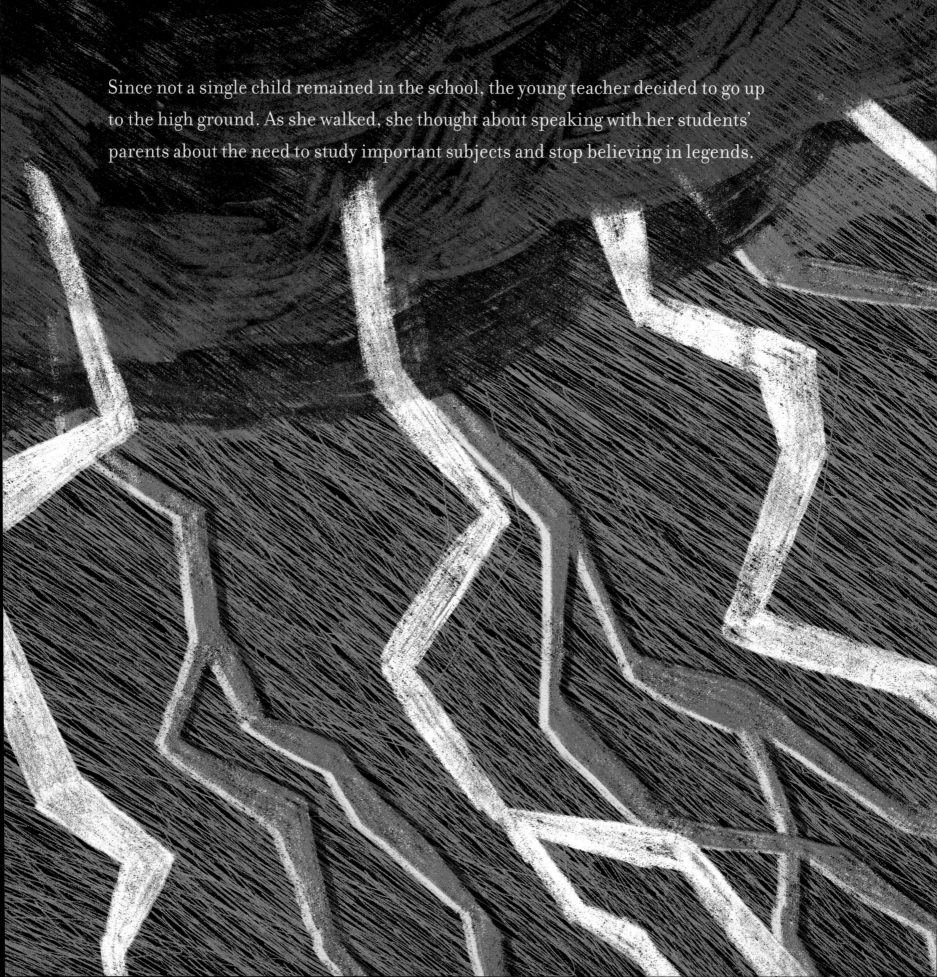

Since not a single child remained in the school, the young teacher decided to go up to the high ground. As she walked, she thought about speaking with her students' parents about the need to study important subjects and stop believing in legends.

She soon noticed
how the sky darkened
and the thunder
and the lightning
multiplied
with every passing minute.

She was stunned and felt afraid.

On the top of the hill,
she found all
the people
of Las Delicias,
and she felt better.

Suddenly, a collective murmur made her look down.
The river—swollen, overflowing, impetuous—had turned into a
great serpent of mud that carried off everything it found in its path.
In a few minutes, in the lowlands, every house, crop, animal, and even
the school had disappeared beneath the waters and the sludge.

"My books, my books!
I have to rescue my books!"
was the young teacher's first impulse.
Nobody paid her any attention.

The next day, although it was still raining, the land was clean and renewed. Nonetheless, the young teacher couldn't stop crying. What was she going to do now without her books?

Then she saw that a good portion of the community had gathered in front of her little room. With great surprise, she saw that the women had embroidered beautiful images on squares of white fabric. The children, in turn, collected the cloth squares and sewed them together. To the young teacher, it seemed like they were making books.

That night, gathered around the heat of the fire and hoping that the rains would pass and the river would return to its channel, the women told stories. They spoke and sang while they passed the pages of the cloth books. Since the young teacher didn't understand the women's words, the children translated the legends and the sacred stories of the inhabitants of Las Delicias.

Even without letters, their books spoke of jaguars, spirits, multicolored birds, chieftains with feathered crowns, parrots, and princesses adorned with lovely, jeweled necklaces and belts.

A few days later, thanks to the work of the entire community, Las Delicias had a new school with a tiny library.

It was built from bamboo and palm, with a new blackboard and chairs. And, of course, with a special place for the cloth books which, day by day, multiplied thanks to the hands of the community's embroiderers and storytellers.

Since that day, the school's most important class has been about legends.

The teacher asked the mothers and grandmothers to come every morning and tell the histories of their community. What's more, the young teacher learned the language of Las Delicias, thanks to the children, and the women taught her how to embroider.

The teacher cultivated the art of making cloth books, and that was how the inhabitants of Las Delicias learned her stories, too, and what she felt in her heart.

The young teacher loved the cloth books. If the rain ever wets them, they'll be dry again soon.

Just like what happens with this lovely land that guards so many mysteries and legends, along the largest river in the world.

The Amazon, kingdom of words and of life:

The young teacher
wanted to stay forever.

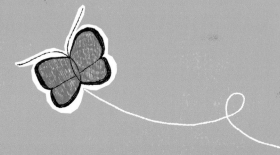

IRENE VASCO is a Colombian children's writer, translator, and educator. For many years, she has conducted reading workshops and programs in remote Indigenous and agricultural communities. In 2021, the Colombian Ministry of Education recognized Irene's career with its "Life and Work" distinction. Follow Irene on Instagram @irene_vasco or visit her website at irenevasco.com.

JUAN PALOMINO is a prolific Mexican illustrator who started his own illustration teaching program at the National Autonomous University of Mexico. His books have received awards at the Guadalajara and Bologna Book Fairs, and the original edition of *The Young Teacher and the Great Serpent* was selected for the 2020 Fundación Cuatrogatos Award list. Follow Juan on Instagram @juanpalomino.ilustrador.

LAWRENCE SCHIMEL has written or translated over 200 books, including *9 Kilometers*, *Niños*, and the Batchelder Honor book *Different* (all Eerdmans). His works have received many awards, including a PEN Translates Award and the GLLI Translated YA Book Prize Honor. Lawrence lives in Madrid, Spain. Follow him on Twitter @lawrenceschimel.

For the older siblings, wise caretakers of the words, of the waters, and of life.

For the Latin American teachers, who give up everything to pursue the dream of education.

In memory of Luz María Chapela and Marta Sastrías, friends and teachers, who taught me so much.

—I. V.

For Ana, who showed me the rainforest.

—J. P.

Text © 2019 Irene Vasco
Illustrations © 2019 Juan Carlos Palomino

Originally published in Spain as *La joven maestra y la gran serpiente*
© Editorial Juventud, 2019

This edition published by agreement with Editorial Juventud in cooperation with Ilustrata Agency.

English-language translation © 2023 Lawrence Schimel

First published in the United States in 2023 by Eerdmans Books for Young Readers,
an imprint of Wm. B. Eerdmans Publishing Co., Grand Rapids, Michigan

www.eerdmans.com/youngreaders

32 31 30 29 28 27 26 25 24 23   1 2 3 4 5 6 7 8 9

ISBN 978-0-8028-5617-3 • A catalog record of this book is available from the Library of Congress.

Illustrations created digitally.